First published in Great Britain in 2005
By W.F Graham (Northampton) Ltd
for Lomond Books Ltd, Broxburn, EH52 5NF

© Lomond Books Ltd, 2005
www.lomondbooks.com

ISBN 1-842-04081-2

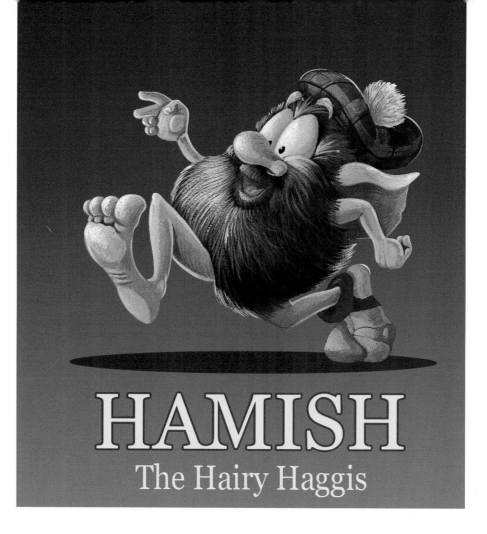

HAMISH
The Hairy Haggis

By A.K. Paterson
Illustrated by Stuart Martin

Lomond

Scotland

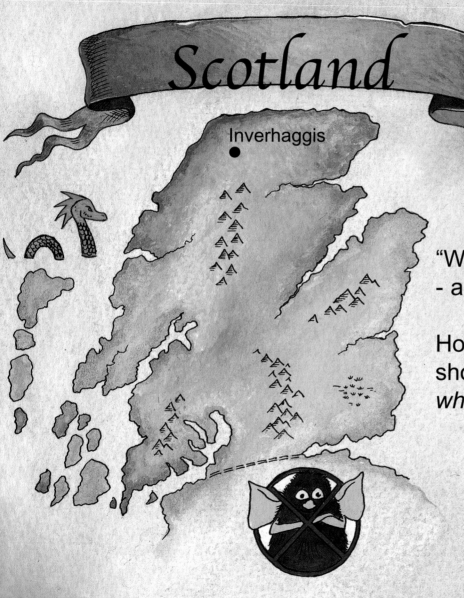

Inverhaggis

"What is a Haggis?"
- a question asked by many.

However, the question should be *not what but who.......?*

It's Hogmanay and everyone in Scotland is very happy. Everyone, that is, apart from Hamish the Hairy Haggis.

Hamish the Hairy Haggis lives on a steep hill in the Highlands of Scotland. The dawn of a New Year means a big, noisy party for nearly all the Scots. For Hamish, Hogmanay is the start of many days keeping his head down hiding in a deep, dark hole. Hogmanay marks the start of the Haggis Bashing season.

Hamish has been in the hole for ages. He has long finished eating all his thistle sandwiches.

Hamish is on the last page
of his one and only book.
He is very bored and very
hungry and wants to go out
to play.

The Hairy Haggis Bashers are usually very noisy so Hamish listens hard at the opening of the hole. It seems to be quiet outside. 'Maybe the Haggis Bashers have gone home for the day,' thinks Hamish.

He decides to leave the hole in search of more thistles to make sandwiches. Big mistake!

As Hamish sticks his head through the hole, a great hammer hits him very hard on the head! The Hairy Haggis Basher had been hiding in the heather. Hamish is in big trouble now!

The Haggis Basher carries
Hamish down the hill and
heads for his home town of
Inverhaggis.

Hamish wakes up and finds himself in a cage. Beside him in the cage are some very smelly turnips called Neeps, and some very dirty old potatoes, known as Tatties. Hamish is a bit groggy but climbs over a Neep to peep through the bars of the cage.

What he sees in the vast room beyond makes him tremble with fear! This must be the ancient ceremony that his grandfather, Harry, the even Hairier Haggis, once told him about -*The Burns Supper*

DO NOT FEED

In the big room, Hairy Haggis
Bashers and Mashers are
dancing together. The
Mashers wear long, colourful
skirts and the Bashers wear
short, colourful skirts.

To his horror, Hamish sees
that one of the Bashers is
wearing his grandfather,
Harry, tied around his middle!

Rabbie Burns, it seems, was the really big chief of all the Hairy Haggis Bashers and Mashers. He was the most feared enemy of Haggis everywhere!

Hamish knows he must escape from the cage. He tries to think of a plan. Then, from the vast hall comes a cry, 'Bring in the Haggis! Bring in the Haggis!'

Hamish begins to shake even more when he
hears these words. On the day of his fifth birthday,
his grandfather, Harry the Hairier Haggis and the
great Chieftain of the Pudding Race, told him all
about the Haggis Bashers and their very
odd ways.

Harry told Hamish that if he ever
heard the words 'Rabbie Burns',
he should run for his life.

The screeching music stops and the Bashers and Mashers sit down at long tables. The chief Haggis Basher stands up and starts to shout loudly in a language that Hamish does not understand. After a very long time, the big chief raises his glass and everyone begins chanting, 'Rabbie Burns!'

Hamish sees one of the Hairy Haggis Bashers pick up what looks like a baby Haggis Basher. He blows on one of its spindly legs and from the baby Haggis Basher comes a horrible high pitched howling!

The terrible noise makes Hamish and the Tatties cover their ears. Luckily for the Neeps they don't have ears, so can't hear the awful wailing.

Hamish remembers something
else his grandfather, Harry,
told him. 'When you hear the
horrible howling - leg it!

'Leg it! Leg it! thinks Hamish,
as he kicks a Neep with all
his strength. The Neep hurtles
towards the bars. It smashes
a hole in the side of the cage
and Hamish jumps through!

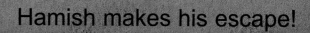

Hamish makes his escape!

Hamish runs for his life through an open door. The Bashers and Mashers chase after him! Meanwhile, the smelly Neeps and the dirty old Tatties also escape through the hole in the cage.

The Bashers and Mashers trip over the Neeps and Tatties. They end up in a tangled and colourful heap.

Hamish is nearly caught by
one of the Bashers, but luckily
Harry, Hamish's grandfather,
springs to life........

.......wraps his legs around the Basher's ankles and trips him up!

Hamish heads for the hills! The Bashers are close behind and nearly catch him!

Hairy Haggis have two very long back legs and two very short front legs which means they can run very fast up hills. As soon as Hamish sets foot on the hill he knows he will be safe!

Hamish is nearly at the very top of the hill while the Bashers are still at the bottom. They are out of breath and very angry!

Hamish sends a traditional Haggis greeting to the Bashers!

A few hours later.....The Hairy Haggis Bashers and Mashers have given up the hunt for Hamish. In the kitchen of the big hall they mix together some very strange ingredients in a huge bowl.

Later they sit down and try to pretend to their guests that this odd, gooey mess is real Haggis.

Hamish warms up some thistle soup. He doesn't have the appeti[t]
for the basher stew.

He is very happy knowing that he is
safe from the Hairy Haggis Bashers
- until next year!

NEWSFLASH

So now you know
the _true_ story
of Hamish the Hairy Haggis!